UNIQUELY WIRED!

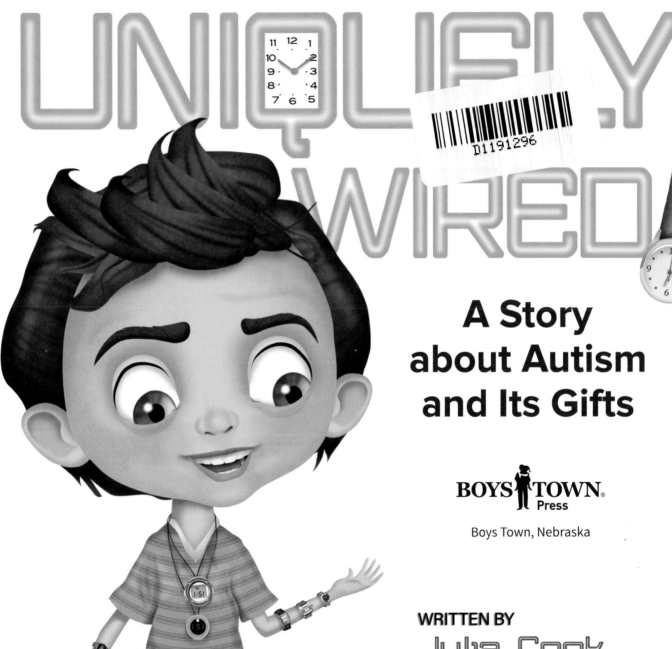

A Story about Autism and Its Gifts

BOYS TOWN Press

Boys Town, Nebraska

WRITTEN BY
Julia Cook

ILLUSTRATED BY
Anita DuFalla

Published by the Boys Town Press
14100 Crawford St.
Boys Town, NE 68010

For a Boys Town Press catalog, call **1-800-282-6657**
or visit our website: **BoysTownPress.org**

Publisher's Cataloging-in-Publication Data

Names: Cook, Julia, 1964- author. | DuFalla, Anita, illustrator.

Title: Uniquely wired : a story about autism and its gifts / written by Julia Cook ; illustrated by Anita DuFalla.

Description: Boys Town, NE : Boys Town Press, [2018] | Audience: K-6th grade. | Summary: Zak has autism, so he sometimes responds to the world around him in unconventional ways. As he describes his point of view, young readers gain a better understanding of his behaviors and learn valuable lessons about patience, tolerance and understanding.-- Publisher.

Identifiers: ISBN: 978-1-944882-19-8

Subjects: LCSH: Autism--Juvenile fiction. | Autistic children--Juvenile fiction. | Children with autism spectrum disorders--Juvenile fiction. | Interpersonal relations in children--Juvenile fiction. | Toleration--Juvenile fiction. | Friendship--Juvenile fiction. | Bullying--Prevention--Juvenile fiction. | Children--Life skills guides. | CYAC: Autism--Fiction. | Interpersonal relations-- Fiction. | Toleration--Fiction. | Friendship--Fiction. | Bullying--Prevention--Fiction. | Conduct of life. | BISAC: JUVENILE FICTION / Social Themes / Special Needs. | JUVENILE FICTION / Social Themes / New Experience. | JUVENILE FICTION / Social Themes / Friendship. | JUVENILE NONFICTION / Social Topics / Special Needs. | JUVENILE NONFICTION / Social Topics / Friendship.

Classification: LCC: PZ7.C76984 U55 2018 | DDC: [E]--dc23

Printed in the United States
10 9 8 7 6 5 4 3 2 1

Boys Town Press is the publishing division of Boys Town, a national organization serving children and families.

I am **Zak.**

I have autism.

Some people say I have a disability.
I don't see it that way at all.
I am **UNIQUELY WIRED!**

I don't see the world the way most people do.

I have an incredible brain, and I have a lot of gifts to share.

respect UNIQUENESS

ACCEPT OTHERS

FAIR doesn't mean EQUAL

FAIR doesn't mean EQUAL

BE TOLERANT

FEEL THE WORLD

FEEL THE WORLD

FEEL THE WORLD

FEEL THE WORLD

Watch what you say

GREAT EXERCISE

Organize your brain

MY MEMORY IS AMAZING...

when it comes to things I am interested in. I used to be into trains—
I mean really into trains. It's like I had **TRAIN BRAIN**.

I can tell you **ANYTHING** and **EVERYTHING** about trains.

THE **LONGEST** TRAIN ON RECORD WAS **4.568 miles!**

THERE ARE THREE CATEGORIES OF LOCOMOTIVES:
① PASSENGER
② FREIGHT
③ SHUNTING

THE **1st** TRAIN WAS BUILT BY RICHARD TREVITHICK **IN 1804**

TOP US SPEED LIMIT —OF A— PASSENGER **TRAIN**
SPEED LIMIT **59**

SPEED LIMIT —OF— A US **FREIGHT TRAIN**
SPEED LIMIT **49**

IN *OTHER* COUNTRIES TRAINS CAN **GO** OVER **200 MPH**

A few years ago, I grew out of trains.

Now I'm into watches. I mean really into watches.

I currently own **379** of them!

I can remember everything I ever learned about watches.
When I look at a watch, I totally get lost...

I love to see the hands move.

I ALWAYS know what time it is!

I love to see the gears turn.

I love to see the numbers.

I love to hear my watches tick.

I can be with my watches for
hours and lose all track of time.

{Hey, that's funny!}

When it comes to my watches, I hold them, listen to them, smell them and, if I could, **I would EAT them!**

When I go to bed at night, my watches go to bed with me. Sometimes, I don't sleep. Neither do they.

If you ever want to teach me something, try doing it from a watch's point of view... then, I just might understand.

"Zak, if a **watch falls to the ground,** it might break. Then it won't be able to move because its insides will be broken.

If you don't wear your seatbelt in the car and we get in an accident, your **insides might get broken.** Then you won't be able to move."

You might get tired of listening to me tell you about watches, but I will

NEVER

get tired of talking about them.

"It's not **fair!!!**

How come Zak can take his watches to bed with him, but I can't take my toys to bed with me?"

"Because Zak's watches help him feel comfortable enough to fall asleep. Your toys might keep you awake because you'll want to stay up and play with them."

FAIR
doesn't mean
EQUAL

FAIR
doesn't mean
EQUAL

"Because of Zak,
I have learned that fair doesn't
always mean equal... and that's okay.

Thank you, Zak,
for sharing your gifts with ME!"

Most of the time, I like doing things all by myself. I really don't like to talk to other people, especially people I don't know very well.

I have my very own personal space bubble. I get to decide who I let into my bubble and when.

Once in a while, my teachers have to remind me that other people have bubbles too.

OOOPS!

I don't like hugs very much, but my mom gives them to me anyway. She says I'm like hugging a **prickly~pear cactus**.

Sometimes I hug people at the wrong time. I just can't seem to figure out the hug thing.

Oh, and you know what else?

I hate it when the tags on my clothes scratch my skin.

Oh, and another thing...

I have a hard time knowing what you're thinking and feeling when I look at you, but that's okay. You can look at me and learn how **I think** and **feel**.

And I have a hard time **LOOKING at you** when you talk to me. When I try to do that, too much information goes into my head all at once and it makes me feel uncomfortable.

That's because you talk with your eyes.

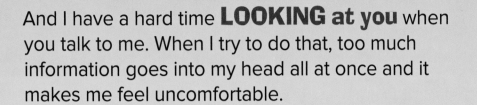

Well, what do you think?

I don't think that is a good idea.

I love you!

I'm not being rude when I look away, I'm just trying to protect myself.

13

I see and hear the world a little bit differently than you do. My eyes and ears are really powerful... like a **SUPERHERO**.

Whenever I look at something, I see all of it all at once really fast... and ***I can't stop it! My brain gets flooded.*** Too much information goes into my head at one time. That's why I have to look away.

Sometimes it's easier for me to

SMELL

things than it is to look at them.

I like to smell just about everything I touch.

I **DON'T** like a lot of noise.

It totally freaks me out. When I hear a noise,
I hear all of it all at once really fast... and
I can't stop it! My brain gets flooded.

I like to wear headphones
to make the sounds softer.

But when I make
loud noises... it doesn't
bug me at all!!

{Hey, that's funny!}

"Zak has the ability to teach us that every person sees and hears things differently... and that's okay.

Thank You, Zak, for sharing your gifts with US!"

17

Sometimes, **I flap** my arms and my hands *really fast.* I LOVE the way the air feels against my skin. Whenever I get excited, upset, bored or anxious, I flap. It helps me calm down my brain and organize what I am thinking.

When I flap, you might think I look weird, but it's just my brain thinking on the outside of my body.

As soon as I feel organized, **I stop**.

You should try it sometime...
it really works! And my teacher
says it's great exercise!

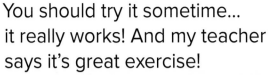

"Because of Zak,
*we're able to feel the air against
our skin, organize our brains,
and get some great exercise!*

Thank You, Zak,
*for sharing your
gifts with US!"*

I am a **SPINNER**!
I love to watch things go around and around and around!

I **SPIN** toys.

I **SPIN** wheels.

I try to **SPIN** everything that I can hold.

And I **LOVE** to spin me!

The faster I go on the outside, the quieter I feel on the inside.

When I spin... **I can FEEL the WORLD!**

You should try it sometime... it really works!

"Because of Zak, *we're able to see that when the world around us is spinning out of control... we sometimes need to start spinning with it!*

Thank You, Zak, *for sharing your gifts with US!"*

FEEL THE WORLD

21

It's really hard for my brain to come up with my own words to say, so sometimes I borrow words from other people... YOU included!

I love to hear myself talk. But once in a while, words get stuck in my brain and then I say them **over and over and over again.** It's fun for me to predict what's coming out of my mouth. I'm like a word copy machine.

If I like the way something sounds, I can make **A LOT** of copies!!!

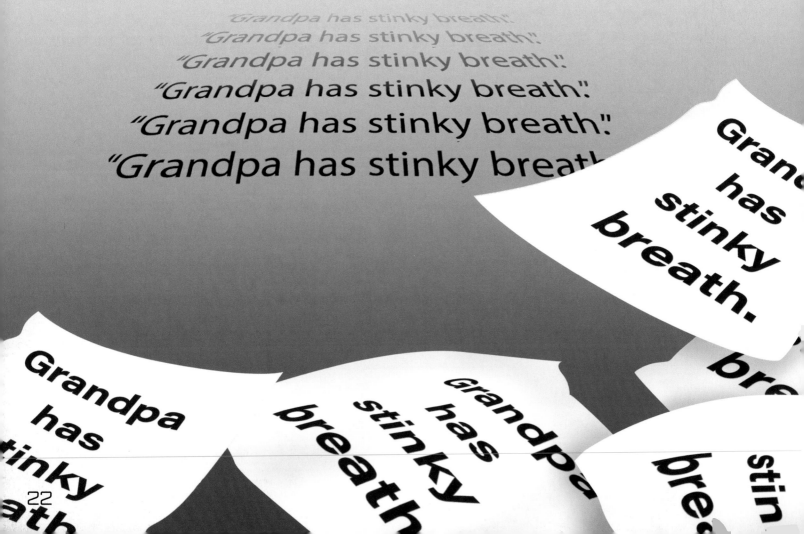

"Grandpa has stinky breath".
"Grandpa has stinky breath".
"Grandpa has stinky breath".
"Grandpa has stinky breath".
"Grandpa has stinky breath".
"Grandpa has stinky breath".

23

"Since Zak likes to borrow words from others, he helps all of us become more mindful of what we say.

Thank You, Zak, for sharing your gifts and making us LAUGH!"

Watch what you say

In some ways, I am different than you, but in a lot of ways **WE ARE THE <u>SAME</u>.**

I feel bad when other kids are mean to me — **just like YOU do.**

I feel alone when other kids don't include me — **just like YOU do.**

I feel hungry, tired, hurt, cranky, cold, hot, thirsty, yucky, and sad — **just like YOU do.**

It's just harder for me to talk about it.

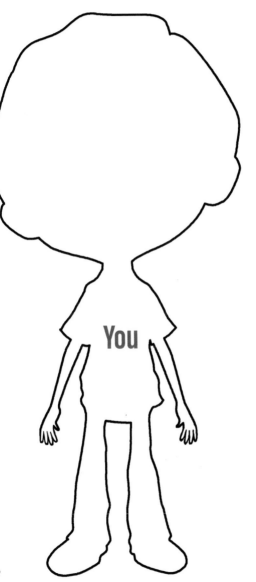

I embarrass my big sister when I laugh at the wrong things, and she thinks I act strange around her friends.

I don't mean to... **I'm just BEING ME!**

Everything I do and say has a purpose. It might not make sense to you, but to me it makes perfect sense. **It's my normal.**

*"**Zak has taught me** to accept the fact that everybody's wired differently. And that's okay.*

Thank You, Zak, for sharing your gifts with ME!"

My little sisters **get jealous** and feel left out because I get a lot more attention from our parents than they do.

I don't learn from watching other people. **I mostly learn from things that people teach me.**

I'm a **black-and-white** thinker. To me, there is no gray in life. So please don't expect me to be able to read between the lines.

Big bag of attention

Big bag of attention

My brain is very crowded and busy, so it takes a lot of **patience, repetition, practice,** and **hard work** to teach me new stuff. I'm super smart in some areas, but I struggle with the little things in life... like getting dressed.

Mom and Dad have to spend a lot more time with me than with my sisters. Sometimes, I just wear them out.

"Zak has taught us how to be more independent. He also has helped us become more patient. Because of Zak, we're better at sharing and making compromises.

Thank You, Zak, for sharing your gifts with US!"

I am **Zak.**

I have autism.

Some people say I have a disability. I don't see it that way at all.
I am **UNIQUELY WIRED!**

I don't see the world the way most people do.

I have an incredible brain, and I have a lot of

gifts to share...
with YOU and
everybody else!

TIPS for understanding children who are

UNIQUELY WIRED!

A special thanks to Melissa Reinhardt, M.D.,
a pediatrician, wife, and mom of three boys (one of whom is uniquely wired)!

1. Children with autism have **special gifts and viewpoints.** Try to see the person within and not be blinded or frustrated by the sometimes difficult or "prickly" outward behaviors.

2. There is a saying in the autism community, **"Once you've met one autistic child, you have met ONE autistic child."** Each child has unique struggles, and the array of challenges is why it's called autism spectrum disorder.

3. **Every behavior has a purpose.** You may not understand a certain behavior or action, but children with autism most likely have a very specific need they're trying to communicate. Over time, watching their patterns, trying to think outside the box, and seeing into their world will help you figure out what they're trying to communicate.

4. Some children with autism have **unique behaviors that are done repetitively.** Many of these self-stimulatory or "stimming" behaviors (twirling their hair or flapping their arms, for example) help them calm down, organize their thoughts, or provide a sense of control. While these behaviors can be disturbing to others or emotionally heartbreaking

to parents, most provide some benefit to the child. It can be helpful to teach siblings and classmates about stimming behaviors to encourage greater understanding and tolerance.

5. **Picking up social cues is difficult** for children with autism. As a result, they may be excluded or treated unfairly. Also, they may choose to hit, push, or scream because they have difficulty processing how to handle feelings and emotions. It can be very helpful to teach and practice appropriate situational responses using visual pictures, including images with faces and emotions.

6. **Teach and engage children** using their latest thing or obsession. If it's cars, for example, animate or humanize cars by giving them dialogue and emotions. Ask questions like, "How do you think Red feels when…?" Or, "When the cars are all stopped at a stop sign, they need to take turns before they can go again, just like I need you to take your turn when you play with your friends or brothers." Or even, "Remember when Red had to go through the carwash to get all that dirt off? Now it's your turn to get in your

carwash [shower or bath] so you can get clean, too!" Also, you can stretch their thinking with questions like, "Yes, I see that police car. Where do you think he's going?"

7. Take nothing for granted... **and make NO assumptions!** You may need to teach your child WAY more things than you ever imagined. **Motor planning** – *knowing what you need to do in a certain situation and then transferring that task successfully from your brain to your body and muscles to actually carry the plan out* – is often VERY difficult and comes more slowly for children with autism. This may be because a child has a deficit in a specific area. It also can be compounded because children on the spectrum don't naturally watch other kids and learn what they do in certain situations. For example, you may have to teach your child to take off his mittens after playing outside in the snow.

8. **Don't be afraid to try something new!** Everyone can use a little push outside of their comfort zones. The first few steps and the first few tries may be rough, ugly, and difficult. But as the new activity or situation becomes more engrained into a child's bank of "this is something I've done before," each additional attempt will be a little more bearable and, eventually, enjoyable. You might be surprised by how much your child really can handle!

9. **Celebrate the wins!** When you work with a child on the spectrum, you get to see and celebrate accomplishments with a fullness and satisfaction that others with typically developing children may gloss over or take for granted – being able to buckle a seatbelt, consistently putting on clothes the right way, being able to open a screen door that requires pushing and pulling at the same time, uttering spontaneous, fluid sentences, or hugging with their arms wrapped all the way around your neck! Those are the moments, the glimpses inside, we live for and need to celebrate.

For more parenting information, visit boystown.org/parenting.

BOYS TOWN Parenting

Boys Town Press Books by Julia Cook

Kid-friendly books to teach social skills

978-1-934490-67-9

978-1-934490-25-9

978-1-934490-58-7

978-1-934490-20-4

978-1-934490-80-8

Other Titles: The Judgmental Flower
Baditude! What to Do When Your Life Stinks!
Gas Happens! What to Do When It Happens to You
If Winning Isn't Everything, Why Do I Hate to Lose?
Teamwork Isn't My Thing, and I Don't Like to Share!

Thanks for the Feedback... (I Think!)
That Rule Doesn't Apply to Me
Cliques Just Don't Make Cents

I Just Want to Do It My Way!
I Want to Be the Only Dog
Making Friends Is an Art!

Cheaters Never Prosper
Peer Pressure Gauge
Sorry, I Forgot to Ask!

Hygiene... You Stink!
The Technology Tail
The Procrastinator

Well, I Can Top That!
Tease Monster
Table Talk

BOYS TOWN Press

BoysTownPress.org

For information on Boys Town, its Education Model®, Common Sense Parenting®, and training programs:
boystowntraining.org | boystown.org/parenting
training@BoysTown.org | 1-800-545-5771

For parenting and educational books and other resources:
BoysTownPress.org
btpress@BoysTown.org | 1-800-282-6657